THE ROBIN HOOD OF KOREA

Anne Sibley O'Brien

Charlesbridge

I CHING HEXAGRAM AND INTERPRETATION:
FOLLOWING/PURSUIT: *NEED FOR FLEXIBILITY AND ADAPTABILITY*

The story begins this way...

Once there was a boy who could not claim his father. KIL DONG, as he was called, was the second son of a wealthy and powerful advisor to the king, Minister HONG.

But KIL DONG's mother was not the noble wife of the minister. She was only a maidservant. Though raised as a son in the same household, KIL DONG was not allowed to call the minister "father."

It was not that Minister HONG did not care for KIL DONG. Before his birth, the minister had dreamed of a great dragon of thunder and lightning. This dream was a good omen for the birth of a splendid son.
KIL DONG was a strong and healthy infant with the mark of a great destiny.
AH HA! HE IS A HANDSOME DRAGON OF A SON, SO STRONG. IT IS JUST AS MY DREAM FORETOLD! AND SEE THIS RED BIRTHMARK? HE WILL BE LIKE NO OTHER.
As KIL DONG grew in strength, beauty, and intelligence, the minister actually favored him over his first son, IN HYUNG.
LOOK AT THAT BOY'S SPIRIT!
But only a son of two yangban parents, those of noble birth, could inherit his parents' nobility and serve in government. Minister HONG could not allow KIL DONG to claim a birthright that was not his.
A BOY SO BRIGHT AND TALENTED, BUT WHAT CAN HIS FATE BE? HE COULD NEVER RISE TO ANY OFFICIAL POSITION LIKE MINE.
FATHER, LOOK WHAT I LEARNED TODAY!
KIL DONG, WHAT ARE YOU SAYING? WHY YOU ARE DISOBEYING ME AGAIN?
HOW MANY TIMES MUST I TELL YOU THAT YOU MUST NEVER ADDRESS ME AS "FATHER!"

Meanwhile, KIL DONG had to watch as his older brother, IN HYUNG, received the recognition that KIL DONG so longed for. IN HYUNG was his father's heir, because he had been born to the minister's wife.

And KIL DONG had to watch as his mother was treated like a common servant.

RETREAT: HOSTILE FORCES ADVANCING, ONLY COURSE IS TO WITHDRAW

KIL DONG turned his sorrow into discipline. Though he had no tutors as IN HYUNG did, he studied from first light till long after dark, reading the classics, ancient history, military arts, astronomy, geography, and philosophy. Everything he studied, he mastered.
But his troubles only increased . . .
WHO DOES HE THINK HE IS?
WHY DOES HE WASTE HIS TIME STUDYING? HE CAN NEVER TAKE THE EXAMINATIONS.
ACTING LIKE A YANGBAN, BUT HE'S NO BETTER THAN THE REST OF US!
HE PUTS HIMSELF ABOVE YOU, DO YOU SEE?
IT'S TRUE. HE GIVES HIMSELF AIRS. HE'S NOTHING BUT A COMMONER.
The worst tormentor was a woman named CHO RAN, one of the minister's companions. She urged the servants on to even more abuse of KIL DONG.
Finally he was unable to endure the daily humiliations . . .
MOTHER, THIS SPIRIT IN ME CAN NO LONGER BEAR SUCH CONSTANT SCORN. HOW CAN I BECOME A MAN IN SUCH A HOUSEHOLD?
I MUST LEAVE.
HOW CAN YOU BREAK MY HEART SO?
I AM NOT LEAVING FOREVER. I WILL RETREAT INTO THE MOUNTAINS TO STUDY WITH THE MONKS, AS IN THE STORIES OF OLD. PERHAPS THERE I WILL FIND A CLUE TO MY DESTINY.

INNOCENCE: MATURE NEW SHOOTS, LET INNER INSTINCTS GUIDE
As the spring morning dawned. . .
The kindly monks welcomed him . . .
YOUNG MASTER, YOU HONOR US WITH YOUR PRESENCE.
and shared their simple food.
With the monastery library and the monks' instruction, KIL DONG continued to study. But some days his heart was so sore that he could not concentrate. He began to wander in the mountains.
One day . . .

The ancient sage (or was he a mountain spirit?) took KIL DONG as his disciple. He began to teach him all the secrets of martial arts, swordplay, divination, the wisdom of the I Ching, the Book of Changes, and . . .
the uses of magic.
And so the seasons passed. Finally the time came for KIL DONG to return to the house of his birth.

But at the minister's house, KIL DONG was still the object of scorn. Night after night, his tormented spirit drove him outside to practice his skills and release his frustration, the frustration that no magic could cure. One night, under a bright spring moon . . .

HE HAS GROWN IN SKILL AND STRENGTH FAR BEYOND IN HYUNG, WHOSE PLACE IN THE WORLD IS SECURE. WHAT IS TO BECOME OF KIL DONG?

YOU ARE NOT SLEEPING? IT IS SO LATE. WHAT TROUBLES YOU?
I CANNOT SLEEP FOR SORROW. I CAN NEVER BE CALLED A MAN.
WHAT DO YOU MEAN?
THOUGH I AM GRATEFUL FOR ALL YOU HAVE GIVEN ME, MY LIFE HAS ONE GREAT SADNESS. HOW CAN I BECOME A MAN WHEN I CANNOT EVEN CLAIM MY OWN FATHER?
HOW DARE YOU SPEAK THIS WAY? YOU'RE NOT THE FIRST CHILD BORN TO A MAID IN A NOBLEMAN'S HOUSE! IF YOU SPEAK SO ARROGANTLY AGAIN, I WILL FORBID YOU TO BE IN MY PRESENCE.
MY REJECTION TORMENTS HIM, BUT WHAT CAN BE DONE? THE LAW IS CLEAR: THE BOY CAN NEVER BE RECOGNIZED AS A YANGBAN. WHAT CRUELTWIST OF FATE IS THIS, THAT SUCH TALENT CAN NEVER BE USED IN SERVICE TO THE KING?

In KIL DONG's absence his enemy CHO RAN had advanced in the household to become the minister's favorite companion. With no son of her own, she depended on the minister's favor to keep her place.

CHO RAN saw KIL DONG's return as a great threat. Without KIL DONG his mother was just a maidservant. But if the minister began to favor KIL DONG, it was likely he would favor the woman who bore him.

CHO RAN began to plot to rid the household of KIL DONG forever.

THAT BOY IS IMPETUOUS AND DREAMS OF THINGS HE CAN NEVER BE. HE MIGHT DO SOMETHING RASH. DO YOU NOT FEAR THAT HIS ACTIONS MIGHT HARM IN HYUNG IN HIS NEW GOVERNMENT POSITION?

She encouraged the servants to make false accusations, which she passed on to the minister . . .

and hired fortune-tellers to tell lies about KIL DONG's future.

HONORED SIR, IF HE IS NOT CAREFULLY WATCHED, HE MAY BRING GREAT MISFORTUNE UPON YOUR HOUSEHOLD.

WHAT WILL BECOME OF KIL DONG? WILL HE ENDANGER OUR HOUSEHOLD?

Unable to sleep for worry, Minister HONG took ill.

At once CHO RAN approached IN HYUNG and his mother.
I FEAR FOR THE MINISTER'S SAFETY. DO YOU NOT SEE THAT IT IS WORRY OVER WHAT KIL DONG MIGHT DO THAT IS THE CAUSE OF HIS ILLNESS?
I AM WORRIED ABOUT MY FATHER'S CONDITION. KIL DONG SEEMS HARDER AND HARDER TO CONTROL. HE HAS DISRUPTED THE ENTIRE HOUSEHOLD. WHO KNOWS WHAT HE WILL DO NEXT?
BUT I DO NOT KNOW WHAT CAN BE DONE.
WE MUST GET RID OF THE BOY BEFORE IT IS TOO LATE.
I HAVE WORD OF AN ASSASSIN WHO CAN KILL A MAN WITH EASE.
LET US PUT OUR WORRIES TO REST ONCE AND FOR ALL.
IT GRIEVES US DEEPLY TO THINK OF TAKING SUCH ACTION. BUT WE CAN THINK OF NO OTHER SOLUTION TO PROTECT OUR HOUSEHOLD.
LET IT BE AS YOU SAY.

FOLLOWING/PURSUIT: ADAPT ONESELF. BASE 9: BEING CROSSED ON LEAVING HOME
Later, on a night dark as ink,
as KIL DONG studied the Book of Changes . . .
CAW! CAW! CAW!
ODD. RAVENS USUALLY DO NOT CRY AT NIGHT.
SOMETHING MUST HAVE DISTURBED IT.
The door began to slide open. Summoning all the magical powers the sage had taught him, KIL DONG made himself invisible. He began chanting a mantra.
A fierce wind sprang up.

Suddenly the assassin found himself in a mountain clearing. The house had vanished. A boy came riding toward him on a donkey.
WHAT SORCERY IS THIS?
HIS POWERS ARE GREAT, BUT HE IS ONLY A BOY—NO MATCH FOR ME!
WHY ARE YOU TRYING TO KILL ME? I AM BLAMELESS.
KIL DONG chanted another mantra, raising a whirling black cloud.
(The following morning the assassin's body would be found in KIL DONG's room without a mark on it.)

KIL DONG went to his mother's room . . .
SOMEONE IN THIS VERY HOUSEHOLD HAS BEEN PLOTTING TO HAVE ME KILLED TONIGHT.
I HAVE COME TO BID YOU FAREWELL.
MY SON, WHERE WILL YOU GO? WHAT WILL YOU DO?
FROM TODAY I MUST WANDER LIKE A CLOUD WITH NO DIRECTION UNTIL I FIND MY DESTINY. PLEASE PRESERVE YOUR HEALTH SO THAT SOMEDAY I MAY RETURN TO CARE FOR YOU AS MY FATHER'S SON.
I WILL PRAY FOR YOU TO FIND YOUR WAY AND FOR YOUR SAFE RETURN.
and then to his father's.
WHAT DO YOU MEAN? WHAT HAS HAPPENED?
ALL WILL BE REVEALED IN TIME. BUT I CANNOT REMAIN HERE.
I SEE THAT YOU ARE GRIEVED. FROM TODAY I GRANT YOU MY PERMISSION TO ADDRESS ME AS YOU DESIRE. YOU MAY NOW CALL ME "FATHER."
MAY YOU ENJOY LONG LIFE AND HAPPINESS, . . . MY FATHER.
Once again, KIL DONG left the house of his birth to wander in the mountains.

story continues . . .

One day . . .
WHAT'S THIS?
THIS IS MADE BY MAN. WHAT CAN IT LEAD TO?
!
HEH, HEH! WHAT HAVE WE HERE?
HE'S NOT ONE OF US. LOOKS LIKE A SPY!
BANDITS!

AYBE HE IS ARRYING ALUABLES.
O WHAT RINGS OU SO DEEP NTO THE OUNTAINS?
HIS CLOTHES ARE IN GOOD REPAIR. HOW DID A BOY LIKE YOU FIND US?
LET'S SEE IF HE HAS ANY GOLD!

WAIT—LET'S HAVE SOME SPORT! IF HE CAN LIFT THAT ROCK, WE'LL LET HIM KEEP HIS TREASURES!

HE'S ACTUALLY TRYING TO LIFT IT.
WE'LL GET A GOOD LAUGH OUT OF THIS!
AT LEAST THE BOY'S GOT SPIRIT!

THIS TASK IS FAR BEYOND MY HUMAN STRENGTH. I CALL ON ALL THE POWERS THAT HEAVEN HAS GRANTED ME.

AIGO-OOO!
OMANAH!

HEAVEN HAS SENT YOU TO BE OUR LEADER!!!
COULD IT BE TRUE THAT THE HAND OF HEAVEN CAN BE SEEN IN THIS? HAVE I TRULY BEEN GRANTED THESE DIVINE POWERS TO USE AS A LEADER OF MEN?
That night . . .
A TOAST TO OUR NEW LEADER!

As the night wore on, the men began to share the stories of how they came to leave home and become bandits.

KIL DONG began to drill the band in swordplay,
SENSE HIS MOVES AND WATCH FOR AN OPENING.
battle strategy,
WAIT HERE OUT OF SIGHT. DO NOT MOVE UNTIL YOU SE
MY SIGNAL.

and martial arts. They trained for months, until they had become a highly skilled and disciplined fighting force.

At harvest time one of KIL DONG's men came to him.
THIS IS MY SISTER. I BEG YOU TO HEAR HER STORY.
I HAVE COME TO PLEAD FOR YOUR HELP. WE ARE DESPERATE.
IT IS THE MONKS OF HAE IN TEMPLE. EVERY MONTH THEY DEMAND TRIBUTE. THEY HAVE TAKEN NEARLY EVERYTHING WE HAVE. IF WE GIVE ANY MORE WE WILL HAVE NOTHING LEFT FOR THE WINTER.
CAN WE NOT RIGHT THIS INJUSTICE?
IT IS WRONG FOR MONKS TO HOARD WEALTH AT THE EXPENSE OF THE PEOPLE.
KIL DONG called his men together.
WE HAVE TRAINED FOR MANY MONTHS. LET US NOW PUT OUR FORCE TO GOOD USE AND TEACH THESE GREEDY MONKS A LESSON. WHAT DO YOU SAY?
WE ARE READY!
HOW WILL WE ENTER?
THE TEMPLE WALLS ARE THICK AND THE GATES ARE GUARDED.
I THINK I KNOW HOW WE MAY GET THROUGH THE GATES. LET US SEE IF MY PLAN WILL WORK.

As autumn leaves turned to flame, a young man rode up to HAE IN Temple. By his bearing, his clothing, and his retinue of servants, the guards knew him to be the son of a nobleman, so they opened the gates to admit him.

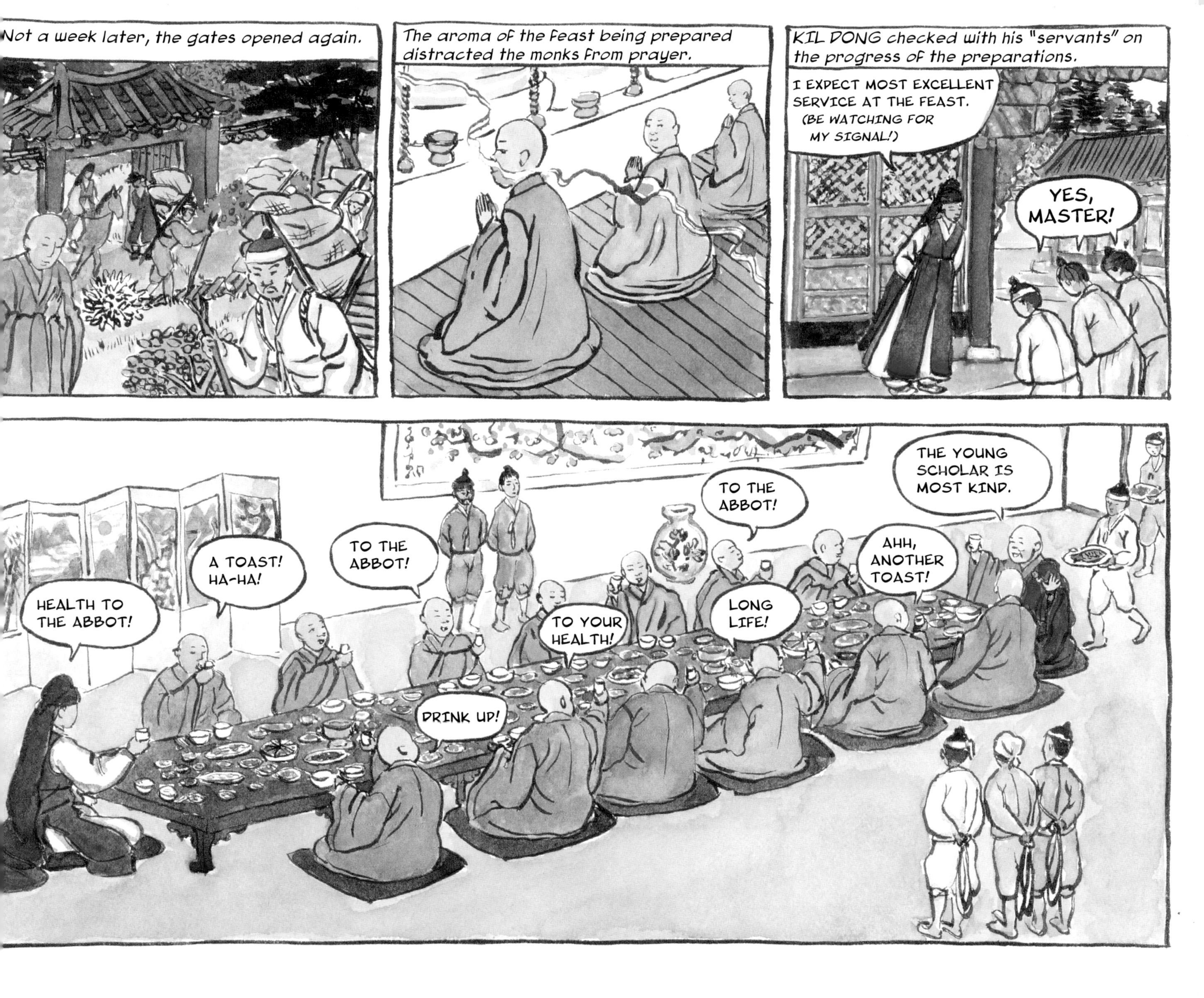
Not a week later, the gates opened again.
The aroma of the feast being prepared distracted the monks from prayer.
KIL DONG checked with his "servants" on the progress of the preparations.
I EXPECT MOST EXCELLENT SERVICE AT THE FEAST. (BE WATCHING FOR MY SIGNAL!)
YES, MASTER!
HEALTH TO THE ABBOT!
A TOAST! HA-HA!
TO THE ABBOT!
DRINK UP!
TO YOUR HEALTH!
TO THE ABBOT!
LONG LIFE!
AHH, ANOTHER TOAST!
THE YOUNG SCHOLAR IS MOST KIND.

When the monks were dazed with food and drink, KIL DONG slipped a few grains of sand from his pocket to his mouth.
STONES IN MY RICE? WHAT AN OUTRAGE! IS THIS HOW YOU SHOW YOUR GRATITUDE FOR MY GIFTS?
At this signal, KIL DONG's men rushed forward and tied up the monks, who were too befuddled to protest.
AIGO-OOO!
!
Others rushed to the gates and let in the rest of KIL DONG's men. All gathered up the stored food, treasures, gold, and ill-gotten gains that the monks had stolen from the people.
A kitchen boy ran to the local magistrate . . .
BANDITS HAVE ROBBED THE TEMPLE!
who sent troops in pursuit
Dressed in monk's robes, KIL DONG stood atop a hill and directed the troops.
THE BANDITS HAVE GONE NORTH! HURRY!!
FOLLOWING/PURSUIT: A MAN MUST LEARN TO SERVE BEFORE HE CAN RULE

KIL DONG directed his men to immediately begin to distribute the recovered wealth to the people who had suffered under the greedy monks.
RICE FOR THE WINTER.
OH SIR! YOU HAVE SAVED US.
THANK YOU, SIR.
BLESSINGS ON YOU, GOOD MEN.
When news of the successful raid spread, other men joined KIL DONG's band.
FROM THIS DAY WE WILL BE CALLED THE HWAL BIN DANG, THE SAVE-THE-POOR ARMY. OUR MISSION IS TO RID THE COUNTRY OF INJUSTICE. WHEN THE PEOPLE SUFFER, LET US HEAR OF IT.
As the cry of wild geese filled the skies, two men appeared from the north.
WE HAVE COME ALL THE WAY FROM THE CAPITAL OF HAM GYUNG PROVINCE. THERE THE GOVERNOR HAS STOCKPILED GRAIN BUT WILL GIVE NONE TO THE HUNGRY PEOPLE. AND HE HAS RAISED THE TAXES AGAIN. YOU ARE OUR ONLY HOPE.

With the first snowfall of winter, KIL DONG's men slipped into the northern city. Under the cover of darkness, several of them crept to the south gate where they set fire to the dry fields.

Soldiers, guards, and citizens rushed to put out the fires.
FIRE AT THE SOUTH GATE!
Meanwhile KIL DONG's army swarmed in through the north gate.
HERE ARE THE GOVERNOR'S STOREHOUSES!
As the men left town, they distributed the stolen wealth to the poor.
The next morning, finding his warehouses empty, the enraged governor dispatched his troops in pursuit.
THIS IS THE DOING OF HONG KIL DONG AND HIS HWAL BIN DANG! FIND AND DESTROY THEM!
But KIL DONG used his magical powers and all his army escaped far to the south.

HONG KIL DONG AND HIS BANDITS EMPTIED A NEARBY GOVERNOR'S WAREHOUSE!
THERE IS A REWARD FOR THEIR CAPTURE.
MAY THEY NEVER BE CAUGHT!
YOUR TOWN OFFICIALS MUST BE NERVOUS, TOO.
YES, THE POWERFUL STEAL FROM THE POOR HERE AS WELL.
The story goes on . . .
As cherry blossoms scented the spring air, word of the daring exploits of HONG KIL DONG and his army spread across the kingdom.
YOU CAN'T CATCH ME. I'M HONG KIL DONG!
THEY SAY THE TAXES ARE BEING RAISED AGAIN.
I DON'T KNOW HOW WE WILL SURVIVE THE WINTER.
MAYBE THE HWAL BIN DANG WILL SAVE US.
LET'S PLAY HWAL BIN DANG!
I'M THE HERO, HONG KIL DONG!
I'M THE GREEDY GOVERNOR, STEALING THE PEOPLE'S FOOD!
JUNG-HEE VISITED HER COUSIN IN HAM GYUNG PROVINCE. THEY RECEIVED RICE FOR THE WINTER.
SO THEY TRULY ARE THE SAV THE-POOR ARMY!

THERE IS CHAOS EVERYWHERE. HONG KIL DONG MUST BE STOPPED. THERE IS SERIOUS TROUBLE BREWING.
ALREADY THE PEASANTS SPEAK OF HIM. HE POISONS THEIR MINDS AGAINST US. HE MUST BE CAPTURED BEFORE ANY FURTHER DAMAGE IS DONE.
OMANAH! CAN SUCH A HERO TRULY EXIST?
IMAGINE THE DANGER IF THE COMMONERS START TO QUESTION OUR ACTIONS! IT UPSETS THE ORDER OF SOCIETY!
I HEAR THAT MORE AND MORE MEN ARE JOINING THE HWAL BIN DANG.
IF THEY RAISE THE TAXES ANY HIGHER, I MAY JOIN MYSELF!

Back at the hideout of the HWAL BIN DANG:
WE ARE TALKED ABOUT EVERYWHERE, AND FROM EVERY CORNER THE PEOPLE CRY OUT FOR RELIEF. WE MUST TRAP CORRUPT OFFICIALS WHEREVER THEY PREY ON THE PEOPLE, BUT TAKE CARE WE ARE NOT CAUGHT OURSELVES. COME SEE WHAT I HAVE PLANNED NEXT.
KIL DONG fashioned seven men of straw. Chanting a mantra he filled the straw men with spirit. All seven men came to life, looking exactly like KIL DONG!
Each KIL DONG took a section of his army and spread out across the eight provinces. On the same day, HONG KIL DONG and his men appeared in the north, in the south, in the east, and in the west.
THE WELL: WISE LEAPER ORDERS SOCIETY FOR BENEFIT OF ALL

eir wrath burning like the summer
n, they challenged corrupt officials
d unfair treatment in every
ovince.
and restored justice to the people.

The alarmed officials sent urgent messages to the court in Seoul to ministers who were also corrupt, asking them to speak against HONG KIL DONG. These ministers came before King SE JONG and filled his ears with lies about KIL DONG and the HWAL BIN DANG.

King SE JONG, a wise ruler who cared deeply about the welfare of his people, issued a decree ordering the arrest of HONG KIL DONG.

FOLLOWING/PURSUIT: ADAPT TO PREVAILING CIRCUMSTANCES

On the same day at the jail in the capital city of each of the seven other provinces . . .
I AM HONG KIL DONG. ARREST ME.
From each province an official brought the prisoner to court, eager to collect the reward for the bandit's capture.
HERE HE IS, YOUR MAJESTY. THE REWARD IS MINE.
NO, THIS IS THE CULPRIT, I HAVE CAUGHT HIM.
THAT CAN'T BE HIM, I HAVE HIM HERE!
THIS IS HONG KIL DONG. HE TOLD ME SO HIMSELF!
PAY NO ATTENTION TO THESE IMPOSTERS. HERE IS THE REAL HONG KIL DONG.
YOUR MAJESTY, IT IS I WHO HAVE APPREHENDED HONG KIL DONG.
THIS ONE IS THE BANDIT HONG KIL DONG. I AM THE ONE WHO DESERVES THE REWARD!
I HAVE FOLLOWED YOUR MAJESTY'S ORDERS AND DELIVERED THE CRIMINAL TO YOU.
THERE MUST BE MAGIC AT WORK HERE.

The king called Minister HONG to court.
IT IS SAID THAT YOU ARE THE FATHER OF HONG KIL DONG. A FATHER ALWAYS KNOWS HIS OWN SON. IF YOU ARE HIS FATHER, TELL US WHICH IS THE TRUE HONG KIL DONG?
FATHER!
YOUR MAJESTY, THOUGH HE IS LOW-BORN, HONG KIL DONG IS INDEED MY SON. I AM PARTLY TO BLAME FOR HIS MISDEEDS, AS MY FAILURE TO ACKNOWLEDGE HIM HAS CAUSED HIM GREAT GRIEF. HOWEVER, THESE ACTS OF LAWLESSNESS CANNOT BE EXCUSED.
KIL DONG! YOU ARE IN THE PRESENCE OF THE KING AND BEFORE YOUR FATHER. YOU HAVE COMMITTED TERRIBLE OFFENSES AGAINST HIS MAJESTY! DO NOT TRY TO ESCAPE HIS JUSTICE.
Suddenly overcome, the minister collapsed. At once, all eight KIL DONGs rushed to their father's side. Each one placed a medicine pellet from his pocket into the minister's mouth.
To the amazement of the court, Minister HONG revived
FATHER, BE CAREFUL, LET ME HELP YOU UP.
CARE AND SOLICITATION FOR THE FATHER AND MIRACULOUS HEALING POWERS. THIS IS NOT VILLAINY, BUT VIRTUE.
OBSTRUCTION: LOOK INWARD TO OVERCOME OBSTACLES

With one voice the eight KIL DONGs spoke.
YOUR MAJESTY, I ASK YOUR PARDON FOR THE TROUBLE I HAVE CAUSED YOU AND MY FATHER. IT IS TRUE THAT I AM THE LEADER OF A BAND OF MEN WHO WERE ONCE BANDITS. BUT WE HAVE NEVER PREYED UPON THE POOR PEOPLE, ONLY SOUGHT JUSTICE ON THEIR BEHALF.

IT IS THE DUTY OF THE OFFICIALS TO SERVE THE PEOPLE. YET SOME OF THOSE IN YOUR SERVICE ARE GREEDY, UNJUST, AND CORRUPT. THESE ARE THE TRUE VILLAINS. THEY DEMAND EXORBITANT PAYMENTS THAT THE PEOPLE CANNOT AFFORD. THEY KEEP THE GAIN FOR THEMSELVES. THEY GROW FAT WHILE THE PEOPLE STARVE.

THESE ARE THE WRONGS THAT I HAVE SOUGHT TO RIGHT. THE HWAL BIN DANG HAS ONLY RESTORED TO THE PEOPLE THAT WHICH RIGHTLY BELONGS TO THEM.
CAN IT BE TRUE? PERHAPS THINGS ARE NOT AS MY MINISTERS CLAIM . . .
IF THIS IS TRUE, THEN KIL DONG IS NO BANDIT.

As they finished speaking, all the KIL DONGs suddenly tumbled over onto the floor. Everyone in the throne room saw that they were nothing but men of straw!
AIGO-OOO!
MORE SORCERY AND STILL HE EVADES CAPTURE!

The story goes on . . .
As grain ripened in the fields, a notice appeared on the city gates of Seoul, signed by HONG KIL DONG.
"THE WONDROUS HONG KIL DONG CANNOT BE CAPTURED BY ANY MAN."
WHAT ARROGANCE THAT BANDIT DISPLAYS! DOES HE THINK HE IS INVINCIBLE?
CAN YOU BELIEVE THIS? HE WRITES:
"THE ONLY MEANS BY WHICH HE MAY BE BROUGHT TO THE KING'S COURT IS TO APPOINT HIM MINISTER OF WAR."
IT IS FROM HONG KIL DONG HIMSELF! HERE IS WHAT IT SAYS . . .
HONG KIL DONG CHALLENGES US TO APPOINT HIM MINISTER OF WAR. WHAT DO YOU ADVISE?
The ministers who had spoken against KIL DONG raised furious objections.
YOUR MAJESTY, IT WOULD BE A COMPLETE HUMILIATION!
WE WOULD BE A LAUGHINGSTOCK TO OTHER COUNTRIES! PERCEIVING THIS AS WEAKNESS, THEY MIGHT INVADE US.
HAVING FAILED TO CAPTURE THIS NOTORIOUS BANDIT, ARE WE TO THEN HONOR HIM WITH A MINISTERIAL APPOINTMENT? IT IS AN OUTRAGE!
WE BESEECH YOUR MAJESTY TO REDOUBLE YOUR EFFORTS TO CAPTURE AND EXECUTE THIS CRIMINAL!
King SE JONG pondered all that he had heard.
DANGEROUS BANDIT OR CHAMPION OF THE PEOPLE? I MUST SEND OUT SECRET EMISSARIES TO LEARN THE TRUTH.
PERHAPS IF HE IS BROUGHT TO COURT AGAIN, I MAY DISCERN HIS TRUE NATURE.

So the king sent a message to IN HYUNG, now the governor of a southern province, demanding that he apprehend KIL DONG at once.
WHAT AM I TO DO? WHILE MY BROTHER EMPLOYS MAGIC, THERE IS NO ONE WHO CAN CAPTURE HIM. WE ARE LOST! I CANNOT MATCH MY BROTHER'S POWERS.

But within a few days . . .
IT IS I, YOUR BROTHER, KIL DONG. DO NOT WORRY ANYMORE. HAVE ME ARRESTED.
The governor knelt to examine the skin on KIL DONG's left leg. There was the distinctive birthmark.
SO IT IS TRULY YOU! IT GRIEVES ME TO MEET IN THIS WAY. AS YOUR BROTHER, I AM SADDENED BY YOUR ACTIONS. WHY MUST YOU PERSIST IN THIS LAWLESS BEHAVIOR? STILL, IT IS TO YOUR CREDIT THAT YOU HAVE SURRENDERED.
KIL DONG offered no protest as IN HYUNG ordered him bound in chains and placed in a barred wagon for the journey to Seoul.

Under the brilliant blue skies of autumn, the procession began the three-day journey to the capital.
THEY HAVE CAPTURED HONG KIL DONG! OH NO!
CAN IT REALLY BE TRUE?
AIGO-OOO!
WHAT A MISFORTUNE!

The common people mourned . . .
WHAT WILL WE DO WITHOUT OUR CHAMPION?
HIS DEEDS WILL LONG BE REMEMBERED.
WHO WILL PROTECT THE HELPLESS NOW?
THERE HAS NEVER BEEN SUCH A HERO!
WE ARE LOST!
while the nobles gloated.
SO THIS IS THE "WONDROUS" HONG KIL DONG THAT NO MAN CAN CAPTURE!
HEY BANDIT! WHERE ARE YOUR MAGICAL POWERS NOW?
WHO WILL SAVE YOU NOW THAT YOU ARE NOTHING BUT A COMMON CRIMINAL?

Then, just as the procession reached the palace gates . . .

When King SEJONG heard the news of KIL DONG's miraculous escape, his mind was made up.
HONG KIL DONG DEMONSTRATES POWERS THAT ARE SUPERNATURAL. IT IS ABUNDANTLY CLEAR THAT HE IS NO VILLAIN. HE SHOWS FILIAL DEVOTION AND CONCERN FOR THE POOR. HE CONDEMNS GREED AND CORRUPTION. HE ABIDES IN THE NINE STANDARDS AND EIGHT VIRTUES. SINCE ANCIENT TIMES THERE HAS NEVER BEEN SUCH A MAN. HE IS TRULY A CHAMPION BLESSED BY HEAVEN. I HEREBY APPOINT HONG KIL DONG TO THE POSITION OF MINISTER OF WAR.
As the last winds of winter chilled the air, notices were posted on the city gates.
LOOK AT THIS NEWS. THE KING HAS GIVEN THAT BANDIT HONG KIL DONG A HIGH MINISTERIAL POSITION.
THE CEREMONY WILL BE HELD IN TWO DAYS.
DID YOU HEAR THE GOOD NEWS? WE WILL HAVE SOMEONE WHO WILL SPEAK FOR US
Word spread to the household of Minister HONG.
KIL DONG'S MOTHER! KIL DONG'S MOTHER! YOUR SON HAS BEEN APPOINTED A MINISTER TO THE KING!
IF HONG KIL DONG SERVES AS MINISTER OF WAR, IT WILL BE THE END FOR US!
BUT HIS COMING TO THE PALACE FOR THE CEREMONY GIVES US THE CHANCE WE NEED. WE MUST SEIZE HIM WHILE WE CAN.
LET US PUT AN ASSASSIN AT THE PALACE GATES. AS SOON AS HE LEAVES, HE WILL BE CUT DOWN.
LET US BE RID OF TH MENACE ONCE AND FOR ALL!

On the appointed day, with the return of spring breezes, KIL DONG dressed in the regalia of the minister to the king . . .
and made his way in a grand procession to the palace. He was flanked by officials of the Ministry of War, palace guards, and the troops of HWAL BIN DANG, who were no longer criminals, but heroes. The people crowded close on every side, trying to catch a glimpse of their champion.
As soon as the procession passed through the gates, a dark figure moved stealthily into the shadows.

HOLDING TOGETHER:
MAN OF GREAT SPIRIT
BRINGING UNION

YOUR MAJESTY, I AM DEEPLY GRATEFUL FOR THIS HONOR. AN ACCIDENT OF BIRTH THREATENED TO KEEP ME FROM MY DESTINY, BUT YOUR MAJESTY'S GRACIOUS FAVOR HAS GRANTED ME MY LIFE'S DESIRE AND FREED ME FROM SORROW.
YOU HAVE EARNED THIS DISTINCTION BY YOUR WORK ON BEHALF OF THE PEOPLE. NOW RISE AND, AS MY NEW MINISTER, GIVE ME YOUR COUNSEL FOR STRENGTHENING OUR NATION.
YOUR MAJESTY, I MUST WARN YOU OF THE DANGER OF CORRUPT OFFICIALS WHO PROFIT FROM THE MISERY OF THE PEOPLE.
I THANK YOU FOR THIS WISDOM. DUE TO YOUR ACTIONS, I HAVE ALREADY DISPATCHED EMISSARIES THROUGHOUT THE KINGDOM. I WILL FIND THOSE WHO ARE UNJUST AND PUNISH THEM, NO MATTER WHAT THEIR RANK.
THE LIFE OF THE COMMON PEOPLE IS ARDUOUS. AS THEIR RULERS WE MUST TRY TO EASE THEIR BURDENS WITH THE BALM OF JUSTICE.
MY PEOPLE ARE FIRST IN MY HEART. I WILL ATTEMPT TO RULE THEM JUSTLY.
LET ME TELL YOU WHAT I HAVE ENVISIONED TO PROMOTE THE WELFARE OF THE KINGDOM . . .
NOW I HAVE ACCOMPLISHED WHAT I SET OUT TO DO. YOUR MAJESTY, I WISH YOU A LONG AND ILLUSTRIOUS REIGN. FAREWELL.
The king told KIL DONG of his dreams for improving the lives of his people.

ith those words KIL DONG leaped high into the air and anished into a swirling plume of clouds and mist.

It is said that KIL DONG and his men sailed to an island where they made a just society with KIL DONG as its ruler, a society in which men advanced by skill and virtue, not by parentage.

But that is a tale for another time.

As for the assassin, he found himself in a mountain clearing, the air pierced by the haunting notes of a bamboo flute . . .

Notes from the Author-Illustrator

I was born in 1952—the year of the dragon.

In March 1960 our family moved to Seoul, Korea, where my parents were assigned as medical missionaries. I was seven years old.

In Korea, I really stood out.

But as I learned the language and culture, Korea quickly became my second home. Though modernization was coming fast, traditional Korean life could still be experienced in country villages.

I returned to the United States for college, but spent my junior year back in Korea at Ewha Woman's University. One of the subjects I studied was Korean painting.

Back in the States, I finished college and began a career writing and illustrating children's books. Over the years I sometimes looked for book ideas in the Korean tales I had heard growing up. I was familiar with the well-known story of the boy hero HONG KIL DONG. One day, while I was doing research at the Harvard-Yenching library at Harvard University, I came upon the novel THE TALE OF HONG KIL DONG, as written by HO KYUN in the seventeenth century, in a book of Korean literature that had been translated into English.

HO KYUN (pronounced huh kyoon) lived from 1569 to 1618 and was the son of yangban parents. His father was a minister, and HO KYUN also served in a government post. But he sympathized with the plight of those who were barred from social advancement because one parent was a commoner. Though fictional, THE TALE OF HONG KIL DONG was said to be inspired by the exploits of justice-seeking outlaws, both historical figures and characters in Chinese literature. It was a reaction against the strict rules of the Confucian society that divided people by social class. These rules determined who would have the chance to learn to read and write. HO KYUN was executed for his alleged association with a group of illegitimate sons who attempted to overthrow the government.

THE TALE OF HONG KIL DONG (Hong Kil Dong Jun) was written about the same time that the Spanish writer Cervantes wrote DON QUIXOTE. HO KYUN chose to write his story not in the Chinese characters that were traditionally used for literature, but in HAN GUL, the Korean alphabet that had been created 150 years earlier. The novel, possibly the first written in Korean, could easily be read by Koreans of all classes. HO KYUN also decided to set the story during the reign of the historical king SE JONG. I love the circle that is made by the first book written using the Korean alphabet having as a character the very king who gave his people that alphabet.

☰ THE I CHING OR BOOK OF CHANGES IS AN ANCIENT CHINESE DIVINATION MANUAL AND BOOK OF WISDOM. ONE OF THE "FIVE CLASSICS" OR FUNDAMENTAL BOOKS OF CONFUCIANISM, ITS POETIC TEXT, AND UNCANNY EFFECTIVENESS IN FORETELLING THE FUTURE HAVE MADE IT A POPULAR SPIRITUAL RESOURCE.

The historical King SE JONG was one of the greatest rulers of Korea's CHOSUN dynasty (also called the YI dynasty). His reign (1419–1450) was a golden age of culture and reform, marked by efforts to better the lives of Korea's people. He passed laws to make taxes fair, so that people only paid what they could afford. He formed a group of scholars, the Hall for the Assembly of the Wise, and supported their studies and research. This resulted in many discoveries, inventions, and advancements, including a sundial, a water clock, and maps of the solar system. He invested in the development of printing, revolutionizing Korea's system of movable metal type, which had been invented in 1403. Many books were produced, including textbooks about how to farm and medical books on treating illness. SE JONG is most notable for instructing a group of scholars to develop an alphabet for the Korean language. Previously, Korean was solely a spoken language, and all writing was done in Chinese characters. King SE JONG's alphabet made it possible for all his people to read and write in their own language.

NOTES ON SPELLING, PRONUNCIATION, AND MEANINGS OF SOME KOREAN WORDS:

When Korean writing is reproduced in English, different spellings may be used for the same sounds. So, HONG KIL DONG may also be written as HONG GIL-DONG or as HONG KIL-TONG.

The vowels in Korean words used in this book are pronounced as follows:
A as in father in the words HWAL BIN DANG and YANGBAN
E as in set in SE JONG
I as in ill in KIL DONG
O as in oh in HONG KIL DONG
U as in fuss in IN HYUNG
The sound of R in CHO RAN is rolled, as in Spanish.

OMANAH and AIGO are exclamations of surprise, like "oh!"
YANGBAN describes someone of the upper social class, someone nobly born.

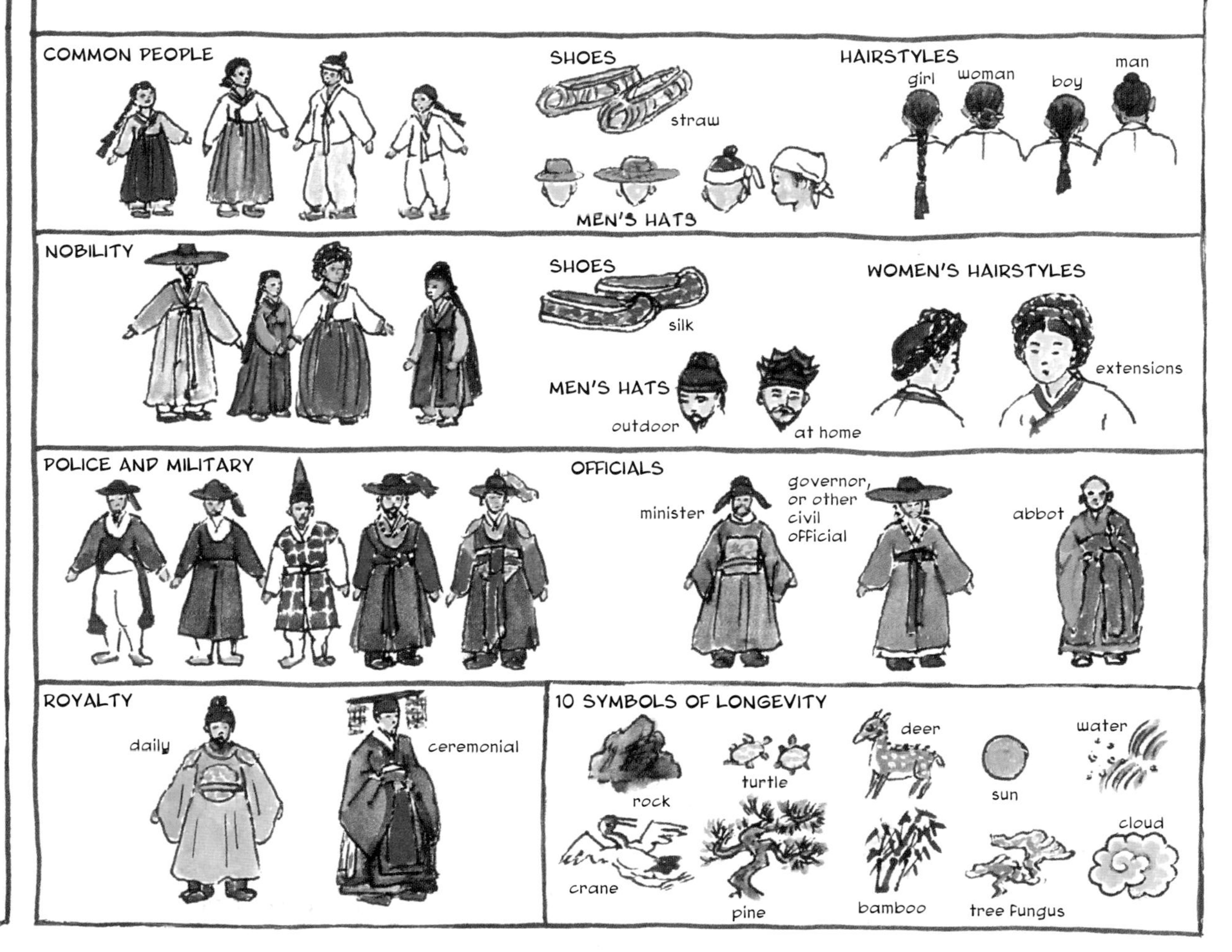

대단히 감사합니다!

With deep thanks to those who gave me invaluable assistance with references, information, inspiration, and encouragement:

CHOONG NAM YOON, Librarian, and HYANG KOOK LEE, Library Assistant, the Korean collection, Harvard-Yenching Library, Harvard University
SOUNG-HWAON KIM of the Kyonggi Provincial Museum, Korea
DAVID MCCANN, Korea Foundation Professor of Korean Literature, Harvard University;
BRUCE FULTON, Young-Bin Min Professor of Korean Literature and Literary Translation, Department of Asian Studies, University of British Columbia
WON BAE and ID BOON PARK
CHON YE TAYLOR and JEONG KYO YOON
PHOEBE YEH and JUDY O'MALLEY
SUSAN SHERMAN and DENNIS O'REILLY

And to my family for all their love and support, with particular thanks to Yunhee, O. B., and Perry.

Sources

The English version of the tale that I found at the Harvard-Yenching Library is The Tale of Hong Kil Tong, *translated by Marshall Pihl, in Peter Lee's 1981* Anthology of Korean Literature: From Early Times to the Nineteenth Century *(Honolulu: University of Hawaii, 1981).*

I also used a Korean text with English footnotes found i Korean Literary Reader with a Short History of Korean Literature *by Doo Soo Suh (Seoul: Dong-A Publishing, 1965).*

My primary source for clothing references was Kwon Oh-Chang's beautiful book, Korean Costumes During the Chosun Dynasty *(Seoul: Hyunam Publishing, 1998).*

A chapter on Ho Kyun in Kim Kichung's An Introduction to Classical Korean Literature: From Hyangga to P'ansori *(Armonk, N.Y.: M. E. Sharpe, 1996, pp. 141-157) gave me important insights into the author's character and concerns.*

All of these sources, and many others I found useful, are available at the Harvard-Yenching Library, Harvard University.

2008 FIRST PAPERBACK EDITION

PUBLISHED BY CHARLESBRIDGE
85 MAIN STREET
WATERTOWN, MA 02472
(617) 926-0329
WWW.CHARLESBRIDGE.COM

LIBRARY OF CONGRESS CATALOGING-IN-PUBLICATION DATA

O'BRIEN, ANNE SIBLEY.
THE LEGEND OF HONG KIL DONG, THE ROBIN HOOD OF KOREA / ANNE SIBLEY O'BRIEN.
P. CM.
BASED ON A CLASSIC TALE FROM EARLY 17TH CENTURY KOREA.
INCLUDES BIBLIOGRAPHICAL REFERENCES.

ISBN 978-1-58089-302-2 (REINFORCED FOR LIBRARY USE)
ISBN 978-1-58089-303-9 (SOFTCOVER)

1. GRAPHIC NOVELS. I. TITLE.
PN6727.O27T36 2006
741.5--DC22 2005056941

PRINTED IN SINGAPORE

(HC) 10 9 8 7 6 5 4 3 2
(SC) 10 9 8 7 6 5 4 3 2 1

ILLUSTRATIONS DONE IN INK AND WATERCOLOR ON ARCHES PAPER
DISPLAY TYPE SET IN LINOTYPE'S VISIGOTH
TEXT TYPE SET IN BLAMBOT COMICS FONTS, DESIGNED BY NATE PIEKOS
COLOR SEPARATIONS BY CHROMA GRAPHICS, SINGAPORE
PRINTED AND BOUND BY IMAGO
PRODUCTION SUPERVISION BY BRIAN G. WALKER
DESIGNED BY SUSAN MALLORY SHERMAN

THE PAGES OF *HONG KIL DONG* AT THE FRONT AND BACK OF THE BOOK ARE A FACSIMILE REPRODUCTION OF AN ARCHAIC KOREAN WOODBLOCK EDITION.